THE KING'S EARS

Published with the aid
of the Arts Council of Wales.

ISBN: 0-86381-394-1

Design: Alan Jones

Illustrations: Carys Owen

First published in 1996 by Gwasg Carreg Gwalch,
Iard yr Orsaf, Llanrwst, Wales LL26 0EH.

☎ 01492 642031

Printed and published in Wales

STORIES FROM WALES

The King's Ears

Elena Morus
Adapted by Siân Lewis

Near Aber-soch in North Wales there is a fine old farmhouse called Castellmarch. On this very place long long ago stood the castle of King March ap Meirchion.

In Welsh, 'march' means 'horse'.

King March was given his name for a very strange reason.

He had horse's ears!

He had never told anyone his secret. He was scared people would laugh at him. Though he had rooms full of treasure, great estates and fine ships, King March was never happy.

March always wore a crown to hide his ears and let his hair grow down to his toes. One day he tripped over it.

'What shall I do?' he said miserably. 'I'll have to send for a barber, but the barber will see my ears.'

March thought long and hard. He had to find a man who could keep a secret. He remembered old Ifan, who used to cut his father's hair. Ifan was a quiet kindly man.

'I'll send for Ifan,' said King March. 'Ifan can be my barber.'

Ifan came at once to the castle with his comb and scissors.

'Now listen, Ifan,' said the king in a stern voice. 'When you cut my hair, you'll find that my ears are not like other people's. You must never tell anyone about them. If you do, I'll cut off your head. Do you understand?'

'Yes, sir,' said Ifan.

With shaking hands he began to comb the king's long hair. From the tangled knots out sprang two long hairy ears. Ifan had never seen such ears in all his life.

That night in bed Ifan tossed and turned. The king's secret was burning up inside him. What if he told someone by accident? The king would cut his head off.

As the weeks went by, Ifan grew pale and thin. He couldn't eat. He couldn't sleep. In the end he went to see a doctor.

'I've promised to keep a man's secret,' he said. 'If I don't, he'll cut my head off. But the secret is making me so ill, I'm sure I'll die anyway.'

'Don't you worry, Ifan,' said the doctor. 'This is what you must do. Go out into the fields and whisper the secret to the earth. That way you'll feel better and no one will know a thing.'

Ifan walked to a lonely marsh where reeds grew. When he was sure no one was watching, he knelt down and whispered to the earth:

'*Mae clustiau march gan March ap Meirchion* — King March has horse's ears.'

When he got up, his trousers were soaking wet, but he didn't care. He felt so happy.

Next day a piper stopped at the marsh. He was on his way to a feast in March's castle.

'I'll make myself a new pipe,' he said cheerfully. 'A pipe that will sing like a bird.'

He cut a fine reed and shaped it into a pipe. Then he put the pipe in his pocket and went on his way.

March had invited all his family and friends to the feast. The tables were laden with fruit and meat and wine in golden goblets. Everyone was having a fine time, everyone except March.

'This is a wonderful feast, King March,' the guests said. 'Thank you for inviting us.'

'I don't suppose they'd have come if they knew I had horse's ears,' the king thought sadly.

When the meal was over, March called the piper.

'Play me a happy tune,' he said.

'Yes, sir,' said the piper. 'I have made a new pipe especially for you.'

He took out the pipe, stood proudly in front of the king and blew. To his surprise the pipe sang in a crackly voice:

'*Mae clustiau march gan March ap Meirchion* — King March has horse's ears.'

In a panic the piper blew again. This time the pipe sang loud and clear:

'*Mae clustiau march gan March ap Meirchion* — King March has horse's ears.'

The hall fell silent and everyone turned to look at March ap Meirchion.

March stood up. His eyes flashed.

'How dare you!' he said to the piper in a terrible voice. 'Bring that pipe to me.'

Trembling, the piper handed over his pipe. The King put it to his lips and blew.

'*Mae clustiau march gan March ap Meirchion* — King March has horse's ears,' sang the pipe.

March flung it to the ground.

As the piper shivered, Ifan the barber fell on his knees at the king's feet.

'It's my fault, King March,' he said. 'I couldn't bear it any longer. It was me. I told your secret to the reeds.'

He covered his eyes and waited for the king to draw his sword. But March only shook his head.

'Ifan,' he said gruffly. 'You did not break your word. I know how hard it is to keep a secret. I shall not harm you.'

Then the King turned to the people in the hall.

'What you heard tonight is true,' he said. 'Your king does have horse's ears.'

Bravely he removed his crown in front of his guests and waited for them all to laugh at him.

But no one did.

Instead March heard a woman say: 'What a very remarkable king.'

'Yes,' said everyone. 'There's no other king like him.'

And for the first time in his life, King March smiled. He was so happy. His dark old secret was no longer a secret at all.

From that day on he never wore a crown and never grew his hair long. After all he was the only king in Wales with horse's ears and he wanted everyone to see them.

A little help with pronunciation

(NOTE: § represents the sound 'ch' as in the Scottish word 'loch'
Ω is the Welsh 'll' (position the tongue to say 'l', then breathe out), as in 'Llanelli'
rr is the Welsh 'r' (always trilled, as in Scots/Spanish)
Bold print indicates stress

Aber-soch — Ab-airr-**saw**§
Castellmarch — Cast-**e**Ω-marr§
March ap Meirchion — Marr§ ap **May**-rr-§ee-on
Ifan — **Ee**-van (short 'ee')
Mae clustiau march gan — **Mae**-e **clist**-ya marr§ gan